Some Canterbury Tales

Ken Pickering

A SAMUEL FRENCH ACTING EDITION

FOUNDED 1830

SAMUELFRENCH-LONDON.CO.UK
SAMUELFRENCH.COM

ISBN 978-0-573-08077-7

www.samuelfrench-london.co.uk

www.samuelfrench.com

FOR AMATEUR PRODUCTION ENQUIRIES

UNITED KINGDOM AND WORLD EXCLUDING NORTH AMERICA
plays@SamuelFrench-London.co.uk
020 7255 4302/01

Each title is subject to availability from Samuel French,

depending upon country of performance.

Some Canterbury Tales

First performed by The Channel Theatre Company at Trinity Arts Centre, Tunbridge Wells, on 6th February 1987, with the following cast of characters:

The Miller	Tim Diggle
The Knight	Bob Joyce
The Host	Chris Pomfrett
The Pardoner	Raymond Polhill
The Wife of Bath	Kea Horvers
Kit	Amanda Wilsher
Moll	Felicity Shepherd

Directed by Philip Dart
Designed by Wiesia Allies and Vernon Marshal

The play takes place on the road from London to Canterbury

PRODUCTION NOTES

The style of the play is rather like a spontaneous telling of a story by a group of strolling players. All the Company take the various parts in enacting the different tales.

The setting is minimal — perhaps a few trestles and planks — and there's plenty of scope for improvisation. Above all it must be direct and energetic.

The music for the play is available on sale from Samuel French Ltd.

PROLOGUE

A bare stage, except for a sign post—To London/To Canterbury

The Miller enters, singing

MUSIC I

Miller (*singing*)   When April with his showers sweet
The drought of March hath pierced to the root,
And little birds make melody,
That sleep all night with open eye—
Then longen folk to go on pilgrimage
Longen folk to go on pilgrimage.

(*Speaking*) In faith, this is the old road to Canterbury and when I last passed this way Master Chaucer himself was with me. You don't believe me? Then you shall hear how Master Chaucer wrote of me, Robin the Miller. (*He produces a book of* "The Canterbury Tales") Now here it is, listen.

The Miller was a stout carl—stop your groans,
Full big he was of brawn, also of bones;
This served him well, for wherever he came
To a wresting match, he won the ram!
He was short shouldered, broad—a man who never cringes,
There was no door he couldn't heave off its hinges
Or break by running at it with his head!
His beard, like any sow or fox, was red,
And broad as well, as though it were a spade.
Upon the top right of his nose he had
A wart, and thereon stood a tuft of hairs
Red as the bristles of a sow's ear.
His nostrils were both black and wide,
A sword and buckler he had by his side.
His mouth was as great as any furnace.
He was a chatterer, a teller of tavern tales.

Now you believe I was with him, don't you? In faith, what a merry company we were!

The rest of the Company enter riding hobby horses

During the singing of the second verse the "Inn" is set up and the wenches bring tankards

MUSIC 2

All (*singing*)   When April with his showers sweet
The drought of March had pierced to the root
And little birds make melody
That sleep all night with open eye.
Then longen folk to go on pilgrimage,
Then longen folk to go on pilgrimage.

And palmers seek out distant strands,
And far-off shrines in various lands
And specially from each shire's end
To Canterbury then they wend
The holy blissful martyr for to seek
That them hath holpen when that they were sick.

As they enter the Inn, Moll and Kit are bustling around

Kit (*to the Knight*)
Welcome good Sir Knight to the Tabard Inn,
Have you ridden far?

Knight   Indeed, fair damsel, in my time I have,
I was in Alexandria when it was won
And in many lands beneath the sun—
Lithuania, Turkey, Algezir and Prussia,
Granada, Benmarin, the Mediterranean, Russia . . .

Kit   Yes, but today, Sir, have you a long journey?

Knight   Today I rest, and tomorrow I ride to Canterbury.

Moll   Then you shall have good lodging with us here
Fetch him some ale now, Kit, linger not near.

Knight   Ah, good. My young Squire is with me, he is yet in the yard.

Kit   I will go find him.

Kit runs into the Pardoner

Pardoner   Your way is barred, pretty madam, tell me your name.

Moll   These Pardoners are all the same—
Straight from the court of Rome they come
With smooth tongue.

Pardoner   Is this your welcome? (*He sings, using any improvised tune*)
"Come hither love to me!"
Never did a trumpet make half so great a sound
As my fine voice, hark how my words resound!
(*He sings again*)

Moll   He hath a voice as small as a goat's,

Kit   Doubtless you will feed him some some oats!

Knight   Welcome, good Sir Pardoner now, in God's name
                    Where is our host, he is to blame
                    For these damsels' tongues.

Host   Pardon, gentles all, a good wife of Bath
                    Is come with much luggage strewn in her path,
                    To Canterbury she rides forth tomorrow.

The Wife of Bath enters, puffing

Wife of Bath   Three time have I been in Jerusalem, but the sorrow
                    And travail I have here are more than all that.
                    (*She sees the Pardoner*)
                    Who have we here, I pray?

Pardoner   With Pardons from Rome am I come today.

Wife of Bath   I am somewhat deaf, what did you say?

Knight   Madam, he brings relics by my fay.
                    But come and sit at table with me—
                    Thou art a lady of experience, I see.

Wife of Bath   I am a weaver of fine cloth, but now 'tis spring
                    On pilgrimage am I wending

Knight   And I too, to the shrine of St. Thomas I ride.

Wife of Bath   Then I shall travel at your side.

Miller   This good wife who came from near Bath
                    Was somewhat deaf, which was a shame—
                    Of cloth-making she had such mastery,
                    She passed them of Ypres and Canterbury.
                    Her hose was of fine scarlet red
                    And a broad hat like a shield on her head.
                    She had been a worthy woman all her life
                    And had travelled the world. Now this wife
                    Was gap-toothed to tell the truth,
                    And had many lovers in her youth.
                    A footmantle she wore round her hips large
                    And spurs on her feet, as if for the charge!
                    In fellowship, well could she laugh and gossip well
                    And the remedies of love could tell
                    For she knew the art of that old dance!
                    (*He moves to the Pardoner*)
                    Come, Sir Pardoner, try some of this brew,
                    Kit, come hither, what's amiss with you—

Moll   No, Kit, you go serve that good wife there
                    I will attend to this honourable pair.
                    Gentlemen, you see here we have fine company—
                    A Franklin there is also in this lodging
                    And a Prioress and her Priest tarrying

	All bound for Canterbury—
	You must not grow drunk or loud, by my soul,
	Your hands and your tongues you must control!

Miller   In faith, pretty Moll, these words are hard,
Wilt thou come with us—in such regard
Do I hold thee—I tell thee this day
We could have good sport along the way!

Moll   Robin, thou art a naughty fellow indeed

Miller (*to the audience*)
        This Pardoner had hair as yellow as wax
But smoothly it hung like a hunk of flax.
His wallet lay before him in his lap
Brimful of Pardons from Rome at that!
He had with him a pillowcase
Which he said was the veil from Our Lady's face!
He said he had a piece of the sail
From St Peter's ship—where is my glass of ale?
And in a glass he had some pigs' bones
Which he said were relics of saints—but his tones
Were smooth and he could read and sing
In Church like anything!

Miller   Harry Bailey, my host, where is all thy mirth?

Host   Now Lordings truly
You be to me right welcome heartily.
For by my troth, and I shall not lie,
I say this year have I never seen
So merry a company!

Miller   A very seemly man our Host was withal—
To be master of ceremonies in a hall—
A large man he was, with prominent eyes—
There's no more imposing burgher in Cheapside.
Bold of his speech, and wise and well taught
And of manhood he lacked right nought—
He was, indeed, a merry man.

Host   And now to give you more mirth have I thought
And the manner of it will cost you nought!

There is general approval

        You are going to Canterbury, God you speed.
May the blissful martyr grant your need.
And well I know that along the way
You hope to tell tales and to play.
Now if you will give your assent
For to abide by my judgement
And do as I shall say

Tomorrow when you ride on your way,
By my father's soul that is dead
If you are not merry, I'll give you my head!
Hold up your hands without more speech!

They raise their hands

Knight We are agreed, good Sir, say on!

Host This is the point, to speak short and plain,
That each of you, to shorten the way
Shall tell two tales, towards Canterbury—
And on the way home he shall tell two more.
And which of you shall tell the best of all
The adventures which have befall—
Here in this place, sitting by this post
Shall have supper at all our cost!
And I myself will with you ride
At my own cost—to be both judge and guide

There is loud applause

Wife of Bath Good Host, this is granted with full glad heart.
Now fetch us wine anon—

Kit Let me go with you on the way I pray!

Host Nay that cannot be, by no way.

Kit I beseech thee, I long to go on a pilgrimage

Host Who will stay this Inn to manage?

Kit Why, thy wife, who has ever managed thee.

Host Nay, in faith that cannot be!

Pardoner O come, dear fellow, the wench must follow her whim,
Let her come with us, and cursed be him
Who does not honour and guard her.

Miller Behold, I pray, his growing ardour!

Wife of Bath 'Tis right that she could come with us.
Experience teaches us all, and thus
In the springtime of her life she should be free
To rove this earth to find her destiny.

Knight She must learn to be a lady with us now,

Moll A lady, by my soul, O tell me how!

Host Well, I see you are agreed that Kit
Should journey with us. I grant it—
But on this condition only—that she may
Help to tell these stories on the way.

Kit	O thanks, thanks to one and all I say.
Moll	Then I must come too!
Host	No, sweet Moll, you must remain behind.
Wife of Bath	In faith Sir, this is not justice to my mind— Women should not be governed thus by men.
Pardoner	Indeed they should—but for what purpose wilt thou come then?
Moll	To keep thee and the Miller on the narrow way And to see with Kit thou dost not play.
Knight	Have done your disputes, let us have peace Betwixt us all—all strife must cease. 'Tis honour and justice that must decide Whether good Moll should with us ride.
	Mine host, give her leave I pray To journey with us at break of day— Many are the tales of knights and their ladies Which we must tell—we need her with us!
Host	Very well, I see I shall have no rest Until I have agreed to your behest— Sweet Moll and Kit, give me your hands— We will journey together—the bargain stands!
	And now to rest we go each one, Without any longer tarrying.

They all go to bed—ie. the two serving wenches unroll a vertical sheet and all are seen asleep with their heads sticking out

Miller (*in a loud stage whisper*)
> On the morrow, when daylight began to spring
> Up rose our host, and was like the morning cock
> And gathered us together in a flock.

Host   Awake, awake, good friends, to Canterbury we must wend.

The Host wakes them and they reluctantly mount their horses and ride round the stage—they then stop together and rein in the horses. Optional repeat of Music 2

> Lordships, hearken if you will—
> Now draw lots from these straws so thin.
> He which hath the shortest shall begin.
> Sir Knight—my Master and my Lord—
> Now draw your lot, for that is mine word.

The Knight draws a straw

> Come the rest of you, lay to your hands everyone!

There is much scuffling as the Miller hopes to have the longest straw but finds that the Knight has won

Knight   Since I shall begin the game
Welcome to be lot in God's name—
So let us ride and hearken what I say.

They all ride off

The Wife of Bath lingers

Wife of Bath (*to the audience*)
This Knight was a worthy man
That from the time that he first began
To ride out, he loved chivalry,
Truth and honour, freedom and courtesy.
Full worthy he was in his Lord's war—
No man had ridden further nor done more
In Christendom and in heathen lands.
And yet no villainy be spoke in any wight
He was a truly perfect, gentle Knight!

THE KNIGHT'S TALE

From this point onwards anyone can play any part in the tales. The story is sometimes acted out during a narration

Knight   Once upon a time, as old stories tell us
There was a Duke that hight Theseus.
Of Athens he was lord and governor
And in his time such a conqueror
That greater there was none under the sun.
Against the Amazon Queen Hippolyta he had won
And made her his wife in his country
And brought also her young sister Emily.

When this valiant Duke Theseus
Had also conquered the city of Thebes—
He took his rest on the battle field
To see what spoils the war would yield.

A pile of bodies is formed

Searching through the piles of bodies dead
They found two young Knights who sorely bled.
They were still alive and their armour fine
Showed they were sons of a royal line.
One was named Palamon
Arcite the other.

Theseus   Take them to Athens, to my strong prison
For these two sons I take no ransom!

Theseus exits with the court

The two Knights are left alone in jail

Knight   And in a tower, in anguish and woe
They stayed—I tell you so.
This passed year by year and day by day
Till it fell out on a morn of May,
That Emily, who was fairer to be seen
Than is the lily upon its stalk green,
Was awake and already dressed
To gather flowers and sing like an angel blessed.

Emily appears and gathers flowers, singing

MUSIC 3

Emily

When I see blossoms thronging
And hear the birds at song,
Then with a sweet love longing,
My heart is pierced and stung,
All for a love that's new,
And yet so sweet and true.
It gladdens all my song
And I know certainly
My joy and ecstasy
To him alone belong.

See Score for optional second verse

The Jailer enters and wakes Palamon

Jailer

Come Sir Palamon, bright is the sun
And clear is the morning,
Rise and walk in your chamber high
From which you can the garden espy!

Palamon gets up and begins to walk up and down—he moans to himself as Emily continues singing

Palamon

Alas that I was born. (*He spots Emily—he cries out*) Ah! (*He almost faints*)

Arcite (*waking*)

My cousin, what aileth thee
That art so pale and death-like to see?
Why did you cry out? Who hath done thee offence?
For God's love, resign yourself to this prison in patience.

Palamon

Cousin, this prison caused me not to cry
I was hurt just now through my eye
Into my heart, that will my undoing be—
The fairness of that lady that I see
Yonder in the garden roaming to and fro
Is the cause of my crying and my woe.
I know not if she is a woman, or a goddess.

Palamon can hardly bring himself to look. Arcite rushes to the "window" and is equally affected by the sight of Emily

Arcite (*sighing*)

That fresh beauty slayeth me suddenly—
Unless I have some mercy and grace
From her that roameth in yonder place.
I am but dead!

Palamon   Do you say this seriously or as a joke?

Arcite   It was in earnest that I spoke!

Palamon (*furiously*)
>   Listen Arcite, we made a vow,
>   That neither of us in love would hinder the other
>   Remember this dear brother,
>   I loved her first and told you my woe,
>   I tell thee, false Arcite, this is so.

Arcite (*proudly*)
>   Thou shalt be false rather than I;
>   And thou art false, I tell thee utterly.
>   For as a woman I loved her first, I vow.
>   You said you were uncertain, even now,
>   Whether she was a woman or goddess—
>   Don't you know what the old proverb says—
>   All's fair in love!

They fight

>   Love her if you wish, for I love and ever shall,
>   And truly, dear brother, this is all.
>   Here in this prison we must endure,
>   And each one take his chance.

They sulk

   Theseus enters with a Messenger

Theseus (*to the Messenger*)
>   I have received a supplication
>   From an old friend that I would release from detention
>   Arcite. This is granted.

The Messenger runs to the Jailer who in turn goes to the prison with a letter

Jailer   Sir Arcite—you are to be set free.
>   (*Reading*)
>   But if thou art found henceforth in any country
>   Of Duke Theseus, then you are dead;
>   With a sharp sword thou wilt lose thy head!

Arcite   Alas, the day that I was born!
>   Now is my prison worse than before,
>   O brother Palamon
>   Yours is the victory in this adventure,
>   Most happily in prison you can endure—
>   In prison certainly, but in paradise,
>   For so hath fortune turned the dice.
>   You will have the sight of her,
>   I only the absence.
>   It is possible that you may win her by some ploy,
>   Farewell my life, my lust, my joy!

   Arcite is led away

Palamon (*calling after Arcite*)
> Alas Arcite
> Of all our strife, God knows the fruit is there.
> Now you are free in Thebes I fear.
> You can bring an army here
> And by some chance or some treaty
> Thou mayest have for lady and wife
> For whom I must needs lose my life!
> (*He sinks down*)

Knight (*to the audience*)
> You lovers, I ask you this question
> Who has the worse—Arcite or Palamon.
> The one may see his lady day by day
> But in prison must dwell always.
> The other where he wishes may ride or go
> But see his lady shall he never mo?
> You decide as you like—and we shall see
> Arcite after two years in that far country.

Arcite enters—he mopes around, writing Emily's name all over the place

Arcite
> For two years I have endured this woe
> I am so weary. (*He looks at himself in a mirror*)
> What is this? I have changed colour,
> (*Sighing*) All haggard and pale, I see in this mirror
> A different face. Although this sickness hath brought me
>   low,
> I could now live in Athens, and no-one will know!
> Squire, help me to disguise myself as a poor labourer!

A young Squire enters and gives Arcite tatty old clothes

The Squire and Arcite both don the old clothes

Squire
> To Athens he went the quickest way
> And to the Court went upon a day,
> And at the gate he offered his service
> To fetch and carry whatever men devised—
> Shortly I must tell you
> He got employment with a chamberlain who
> Attended Emily.

Emily enters

Emily (*to the Squire*)
> What is the name of that young man
> Who faithfully serves me all he can?

Squire
> If you please, I think it so,
> He calls himself Philostrato.

Emily
> He is so gentle in his devotion
> I shall recommend him for promotion.

Theseus enters

Theseus   Philostrato I shall take you higher,
                   And of my chamber make you my squire,
                   And give you gold to maintain your degree.

Arcite goes into a corner and counts money bags and his Squire brings him more

Squire (*to the audience*)
                   And I brought him out of his country.
                   From year to year, full privately, his rent—
                   But honestly and slyly he it spent,
                   So no man wondered how that he it had.
                   And three years in this wise his life he led.

Meanwhile Palamon is still in prison

Palamon   Jailer! Jailer!

Jailer   What's amiss?

Palamon   Let us be friends.
                   I have here some spiced and honeyed wine.
                   Brought by a goodly friend of mine,
                   Let us drink of this wonderful brew
                   To help us see the dark night through.

Jailer   Indeed Sir, this is truly kind—
                   This will soothe my aching mind.
                   (*He drinks and falls fast asleep*)

Palamon now escapes from the prison by climbing out of a window and letting himself down. He may have a friend below who throws a rope up to him

Palamon   I must flee as fast as ever I may,
                   The night is short, it is nearly day.
                   So I must needs quickly hide
                   In this grove which is close beside.

He hides behind a bush that has "entered"

                   In this grove I must hide all day
                   And in the night will take my way!

Arcite enters on horseback, singing

MUSIC 4

Arcite   May, with all thy flowers and thy green
                   Welcome be thou, fair fresh May.

Arcite parks his horse and walks around gathering garlands which he wears and strikes melancholy and romantic poses. Meanwhile Palamon peers anxiously from the bush

(Sighing)   You slay me with your eyes, Emily,
You are the cause for which I die,
Of all the remnant of my other care
I set not the maintenance of a tare—
If I could but give you pleasure. *(He swoons)*

Palamon can't stand this any longer

Palamon   Arcite, false and wicked traitor—
Now are you caught, that lovest my lady so.
You who have duped here Duke Theseus
And falsely hast changed thy name thus—
I will be dead, or else thou shalt die!
Although I have no weapon in this place
But out of prison am escaped by grace—
Be assured that either thou shalt die
Or thou shalt not love Emily!

Arcite *(drawing a sword)*
Were it not that you are sick and crazed for love
You would never go retire from this grove!
But, for as much as thou art a worthy Knight
I will bring arms here for you tonight,
And meat and drink this night will I bring
Enough for thee and clothes for thy bedding—
Then we will fight.
And if so be that thou my lady win
And slay me in this wood that I am in,
You are welcome to her, for all of me!

They shake on it and arm themselves, helped by a Squire

Knight   There was no "good day", nor no saluting
But straight without word or speaking
Each of them helped to arm the other
As friendly as if he were his brother.

They prepare to fight with lances

Knight   And then like wild boars foaming in their mouth
They fought up to the ankles in blood!

They fight

   Theseus enters with Hippolyta and Emily

Theseus   Ho!
No more, on pain of losing your head,
By mighty Mars, he shall soon be dead
That smiteth any further stroke!

The fighting stops

              What men are ye that fight here?

Palamon   Sire, there is no need for words.
                       We have both deserved death—
                       Slay me first for Saint Charity
                       But slay my fellow also as well as me—
                       Or kill him first—though you know not this fighter.
                       It is your enemy Arcite!
                       Who was banished from your land,
                       And came to your gate as Philostrato.
                       And he is one that loves Emily.
                       And since the day has come that I shall die,
                       I confess that I am Palamon
                       That has broken from prison wickedly,
                       And I love Emily ardently.

Theseus   This is a speedy settlement—
                       You shall both die by mighty Mars the red!

Hippolyta (*weeping*)
                       It is a great pity that such a chance befall

Emily   Indeed it is, so think we all!

Hippolyta   For gentle men they are, of great estate,
                       And nothing but for love was this debate.

Emily   To see their bloody wounds both wide and sore—
                       On our knees for mercy we implore!

The women grovel at Theseus's feet

Theseus (*obviously relenting*)
                       Since I know of love's pain, alas
                       I will forgive your great trespass.
                       But, speaking for my sister Emily
                       For whom you have this great jealousy—
                       Ye know yourself she cannot marry two
                       At once, whatever you may do.
                       So listen to my conclusion—fifty weeks from this day
                       You each shall bring a hundred knights
                       Armed for battle, for jousting fights
                       And whichever of your sides shall win the strife
                       He shall have Emily as a wife!

The stage becomes a bustle of people preparing for a tournament. Banners are erected, tiers of seats represented etc

Knight   The day approached of their returning
                       When each of them should a hundred knights bring.
                       There you might see coming with Palamon
                       Lycurgus himself, the great King of Thrace,
                       Black was his beard and manly was his face!
                       And Arcite, as in histories you may find,

Came riding with Emetreus, the King of Ind
Upon a bay steed, with trapping of steel.

Trumpets sound, the Knights appear on horses

Theseus, Hippolyta and Emily take their seats in an elevated position. At a
signal the jousting begins. After a long fight Palamon and Arcite are locked in
conflict but another Knight disarms Palamon and he is left helpless on the
ground and then tied to a stake. Theseus rises

Theseus   Stop, no more! For it is over!
I will be the true judge, not biased to one party,
Arcite of Thebes shall have Emily!

The next speech is acted out

Knight   The trumpeters with loud minstrelsy
And heralds shouted forth instantly
To celebrate the triumph of Arcite
—But then the crowd fell quieter
For listen what miracle befel anon!
Fierce Arcite spurred his fine horse on
And rode the full length of the field
Looking up at Emily.
But out of the ground an infernal spirit arose
And then in panic, I suppose
His horse turned and reared up high
And pitched his rider on his head—
And there in his place he lay, as if dead.
Anon, he was carried from the place
The blood still running on his face,
With sore heart to Theseus's palace
And there he was out of his harness.

A solemn procession and Arcite is carried to a bed—he cries out "Emily,
Emily!"

The breast of Arcite swelled the more
And his wounded heart grew sore—
No drink of herbs could be his helping—
Arcite had to die.

Emily and Palamon approach Arcite's bed

Arcite   To you my lady, that I love most
I bequeath the service of my ghost—
Alas the woe, alas the pains strong
That I for you have suffered so long—
Alas the death, alas my Emily,
Alas the parting of our company.
Farewell my sweet foe, my Emily,
Take me softly in your arms, hear what I say.

                    If you are ever to be a wife
                    Remember worthy Palamon, that gentle man!
                    Mercy Emily! (*He dies*)

        Theseus leads Emily, swooning, away

                              MUSIC 5

Company   Requiem aeternam,
                            Requiem aeternam
                            Requiem aeternam
                            Dona eis, domine.
                            Requiem aeternam
                            Dona eis, domine.

Knight   Duke Theseus with all diligent care
                            Thought where they should the grave prepare,
                            And he at last decided on that grove
                            Where they had first battled for love.

A gravestone is put by the bush

    Emily and Palamon are on opposite sides of the stage

Theseus (*to Emily*)
                    Sister, this is my opinion—
                    This gentle Palamon, your own Knight
                    That serves you with will, heart and might
                    And has ever done so since ye first him knew,
                    Should now receive some grace from you—
                    Take him as your husband and your lord—
                    Take my hand if you will accord.

Emily does so slowly

                    Palamon, I'm sure you need little sermonizing
                    To make you agree to this thing—
                    Come near and take your lady by the hand!

Knight   And between them was made the bond.
                    And thus with all bliss and melody
                    Hath Palamon wedded Emily.
                    And God that all this world hath wrought
                    Send them his love that was dearly bought.
                    And now is Palamon in happiness
                    Living in bliss, riches and healthiness
                    And Emily loveth him tenderly
                    And he serves her just as gently
                    That never was there no angry word them between.
                    Thus endeth Palamon and Emily,
                    And God save all this fair company—Amen.

All applaud and remove any "stage" costumes they have put on. The Miller starts drinking

One of the Company
>This was a noble story
>And worthy for our memory.

Host
>As I can walk, this goes aright—
>Unbuckled is the purse—
>Let's see now who shall tell another tale
>For truly the game is well begun.
>(*To the Pardoner*)

Now, Sir, tell me if you can tell a tale to match the Knight.

THE WIFE OF BATH'S TALE

Miller (*obviously rather drunk*)
By arms and by blood and bones
I can a noble tale for the nones
With which I will match the Knight's tale.

Host   You my friend are too drunk with ale!
Now wait, Robin, my dear brother,
Some better man shall tell us first another!

Wife of Bath   Experience, though there were none other authority
In the world would be grounds enough for me
To speak of the woe that is in marriage.
For, lordings, since I was twelve years of age
—Thanks be to God of eternal life—
Husbands, at the church door, I have had five!

Pardoner   Dame, I pray you, if it be your will
Tell forth your tale as you began
And teach us young men some of your practice.

Wife of Bath   Gladly, since it may you like,
But yet I pray to all this company
That if I speak a fantasy
Take it not amiss—
Now, Sirs, I should say truth that of the husbands I had,
Three of them were good and two were bad.

Pardoner   This is a long preamble to a tale!

Host   Peace, and that at once.

Miller   Damn me, if I don't tell three tales
Before we come to Sittingbourne!

Host   Let the woman tell her tale,
You fare like folk drunk on ale.

Wife of Bath   All ready sir, if I have licence of this
Worthy Friar—I will begin.

Pardoner   Tell forth, and I will hear!

Wife of Bath   In the old days of King Arthur
Of whom Britons speak with great honour,
All this land was filled with fairies.
It so befell that this King Arthur

Had in his house a lusty bachelor,
Who came riding one day and by chance
Saw a maiden,
And robbed her by force of her innocence.
This Knight was condemned by the King to die.
By course of the law he should have lost his head.

King Arthur   Take him away!

Queen   Spare him, I pray!

King Arthur   Very well, have him at your will
To decide whether to save or spill.

Queen (*to the King*)
I thank you, my lord, with all my might.
(*To the Knight*)   Now come before me, foolish Knight.
Thou standest yet in such array
That if thy life hath no surety.
I will grant you life if you can discover and enquire
What it is that women most desire.
I will give you leave to be gone
A year and a day—and anon
You must come back to this place
To give an answer to escape the axe.

Wife of Bath   This Knight was woeful,
Full sorrowfully he sighed,
But he had no choice but forth to ride
And return in a year hence,
So he took his leave and went from thence.

Improvisation sequence in which the Knight rides or walks round asking all
women (including audience) what they most desire

Woman 1   Riches.
Woman 2   Honour.
Woman 3   Happiness.
Woman 4   Rich array.
Woman 5   To be wed.
Woman 6   Joy in bed.

Knight   I've been to every part of this country
But no two women will agree!

Wife of Bath   This Knight, of whom my tale is specially,
When he saw that he might not come thereby,
That is to say, what women love the most,
Within his breast full sorrowful was the ghost.
But homeward bound, burdened with care
He saw by the forest's edge there,
Ladies moving in a dance.

DANCE 1

Women dance. As the Knight approaches all vanish except an old hag left sitting

Old Hag   Sir Knight, no road lies this way,
                   Tell me what you seek, for it may
                   Be better for you if you do.
                   We old folk know many things true.

Knight   Dear mother, most certainly,
                   For I am as good as dead if I cannot say
                   What is it that women most desire.

Old Hag   If you do what I require,
                   So long as it lies within thy might,
                   I will tell you this thing before night.
                   Give me your hand as a promise here
                   And I will whisper in your ear. (*She does so*)
                   Now be glad and do not fear!

The court assembles and everyone gathers round

Queen   I command you all to keep silence —
                   Now the Knight must tell in audience
                   What thing worldly women love best.

Knight   I believe I shall win this test!
                   My liege lady, generally
                   Women desire to have sovereignty
                   Over their husbands and their lovers.
                   This is their greatest desire — now you may me kill,
                   Do as you wish, I am here at your will!

Wife of Bath   In all the court there was neither wife nor maid
                   Nor widow who contradicted what he said!

Old Hag (*jumping up*)
                   Mercy, my sovereign lady queen —
                   Before your court departs justice just be seen.
                   I taught this answer unto the Knight.
                   For which he gave me a promise quite,
                   That he would do the very first thing
                   I asked of him.
                   Before this court, then, as I have saved your life
                   I ask you to take me as your wife!

Knight (*horrified*)
                   Ah, no, alas and woe is me —
                   I know I made this promise to thee —
                   My excuses may sound shoddy.
                   Take my goods and spare my body!

Old Hag   No, for though I am ugly and poor —

                    I want your love and nothing more.

Wife of Bath   But all for nought, the end is this
                    That he was forced to face
                    He must needs wed,
                    And take his old wife home to bed.

The Knight covers his eyes. There are sounds of wedding bells. He carries her over the threshold. She gets into bed and lies there. He, hardly able to look, eventually climbs in and tosses around not looking at her. She lies smiling, quite still

Old Hag   O dear husband, bless my soul,
                    Does every knight so fidget and roll?
                    Is this the law of King Arthur bold,
                    Are all his knights so limp and cold?
                    I am your own love and your wife
                    I am she who saved your life.
                    Tell me what's wrong now, like a man,
                    And I'll correct it if I can.

Knight (*hardly able to speak*)
                    You are so loathesome and so old—
                    Such a sight do I behold,
                    You can't expect my heart to burn
                    No wonder that I toss and turn.

Old Hag   Oh, is this the cause of your unrest?

Knight   Yes, certainly, you might have guessed!

Old Hag   No Sir, I could amend all this—
                    Just look at me and you shall have bliss.
                    (*She winds her arms around him*)
                    Choose now, one of these two things I offer you.
                    To have me old and ugly my whole life through—
                    And to be a loving and faithful wife
                    And never displease you in my life.
                    Or else to have me young and fair.
                    With many other men coming to stare
                    —And there is the risk of losing me.
                    —Now choose, which is it to be.

The Knight gets out of bed and paces up and down, thinking

Knight   My lady and my love and wife so dear
                    I put myself under your control here.
                    Choose yourself which may be most pleasurable
                    For both of us. I am not able.
                    Whatever pleases you, suffices me.

Old Hag   Then I over you have the mastery?
                    Since I may choose and rule as I please?

Knight   Yes, certainly wife, for a life of ease.

Old Hag   Then kiss me and we will be angry no more.

The Knight turns away

                    For I swear to be fair and good. Before
                    You turn away from me
                    Lift up the bedclothes then and see.

*The Knight gingerly lifts the covers to reveal a beautiful young woman. In slow
motion he embraces her*

Wife of Bath   His heart was bathed in a bath of bliss.
                    A thousand times he did her kiss.
                    And she obeyed him in everything
                    That gave him pleasure or liking.
                    And Jesu send us
                    Husbands who are meek, young and lively in bed,
                    And grace to outlive those we wed.
                    Also I pray to shorten the lives
                    Of those who won't be governed by their wives!

The Wife of Bath sings Emily's song (Music 3)—optional

Host   Now, friends, we have heard the good wife's song,
                    Let's refresh ourselves at the inn and meet anon!

MUSIC 7

Company   Our tale is done, our tale is done
                    And God save all the company.

THE PARDONER'S TALE

Host (*to the audience*)
This is indeed an enjoyable ride
But you will have to help decide
Which tale is best;
Now let's hear the rest!
You pretty boy, you Pardoner,
Tell us some merry story, will you Sir!

Pardoner
It shall be done by Saint Ronyon
But first, here at this ale-stake
I will both drink and eat a cake.

They all sit round and dine

One of the Company
Now don't tell us any ribaldry
But some worthwhile piece of morality.

Pardoner
I grant it—but I must think
Upon some honest thing while that I drink!

When I preach in Church, it is always so
I tell them stories of long ago—
For ignorant people love tales old,
Such things they can report and hold.
Now that I've drunk my good strong ale
You wish me to tell you a tale.
By God, I hope I shall tell you a thing
That shall, by reason, be to your liking.
Now, hold your peace, I will my tale begin.

The story is acted out, starting at the tavern

In Flanders once there was a company
Of young folk who spent their time in folly.
In riotous living, gambling, women and at night
They would play at dice until it was light!
And then would come the dancing girls.
And other wenches with seductive curls.

DANCE 2
(Tavern Dance)

Wine is a terrible thing, and drunkenness
Is full of quarrelling and wretchedness—

> O drunken man, disfigured is thy face,
> Sour is thy breath, foul art thou to embrace!
> And I should warn you against gambling,
> The very mother of lies and dissembling!

A bell rings

A body is carried across the stage

First Rake (*calling a servant*)
> Go quickly and ask without delay
> Whose corpse that is that they carry away.
> Be sure to ask the name!

Servant
> There is no need for me to ask
> The meaning of this grisly task.
> He was, indeed, an old friend of thine
> Who was sitting on a bench drunk with wine,
> When this night suddenly a thief men call Death,
> Came and stole away his breath.
> This thief slays all in this country—
> And without a word he goes his way.
> He hath slain a thousand in this pestilence,
> And master, before you came in his presence,
> Me thinketh it be necessary
> To be wary of such an adversary.

Tavern Keeper This child speaks truth for in a village
> A mile away this thief has slain page,
> Man, woman and child.
> I believe that thief lives there, be not beguiled.

Second Rake Yea, is it such peril him to meet?

Third Rake I shall seek him in by-way and in street!

First Rake Listen, fellows, we are of one mind—
> Let us vow this traitor to find.
> *He* shall be slain before tonight—
> We'll swear loyalty to each other in this fight!

They all place their hands on a sword

All Three We vow to find and kill this traitor—Death!

They set out

Old Woman (*greeting them*)
> Now Lords, God protect you!

First Rake What woman, with poor grace
> Why are you all wrapped up except for your face?

Second Rake Why do you live so long, to such great age?

Old Woman   Because, even if I walked to India
                    I would not find anyone, I assure you
                    Who would swap their youth for my great age,
                    Therefore I must keep my age still,
                    As long as it remains God's will.
                    Death refuses to take my life
                    So thus I walk, in endless strife.
                    But Sirs, it is not a courtesy
                    To insult an old woman by the way.

Third Rake   Nay, old churl, you shall see
                    You cannot get away so easily
                    You mentioned that traitor Death just now,
                    You are his spy, to that I vow

Second Rake   Tell us where he is or you will regret it—
                    You are part of his trap—against youth he set it!

Old Woman   Now, Sirs, if you are as eager as you say
                    To find Death, just turn up this crooked way,
                    For in that grove I left him by my fay—
                    Under that tree I saw him stay.
                    See ye that oak, right there you shall him find
                    —Now God bless you who redeemed mankind!

Pardoner   And when they came to that tree,
                    There they found
                    Eight bushels full of florins round,
                    And each of them was glad of the sight
                    Of those coins so fair and bright.

They run off quickly and come to the tree. They find a sack of gold coins and they greedily pass them round

First Rake   Brethren, take heed what I say—
                    My wit is great, though I joke and play—
                    This treasure hath fortune unto us given
                    With mirth and jollity our days to enliven.
                    So lightly as it came, so will we spend—
                    But if to our homes with this gold we wend—
                    We must do it by night and we must be sly
                    So that no-one sees us passing by.
                    Therefore I suggest that we draw lots
                    To see who should go to the town to get pots
                    Of wine and some bread,
                    While the other two guard this treasure instead.

First Rake brings three straws and they draw. Third Rake draws the shortest and goes off to town

First Rake (*very confidentially*)
                    Thou knowest well thou art my sworn brother,

Now we must be faithful to one another;
You know that one companion has gone,
And this gold that so brightly shone,
Must be shared between three.
If it were between *two*, how would that be?

Second Rake   I know not what you intend to do,
He knows the gold's here with us two.

First Rake   Will you keep a secret if I thee tell?

Second Rake   You could trust me what'ere befell!

First Rake   Now, thou knowest well that we be two—
And two are stronger than one, see you.
Look, when he is sat down, straight away
Get up as if a prank you would play.
And I will stab him from one side, dear brother,
While you, as in fun, with your dagger from the other!
Then this gold shall divided be.
Dear friend betwixt you and me!

Second Rake   Then we may both our lusts fulfil
And play at dice at our own will.

They agree and settle down to wait

Third Rake (*walking alone to town*)
O Lord, if only I might
Have all to myself those coins bright
There would be no man living beneath the sky
Who would be merrier than I!
—It is therefore my intent
To slay them both and never repent.

He goes to an Apothecary

Good Apothecary, I pray you me sell
Some poison that will my rats quell,
There is also a polecat in my yard
Who kills my capons, 'tis hard.
Sell me some poison with which to fight
These vermin who attack by night.

Apothecary   And thou shall have
A thing, God my soul save;
In all the world there is no creature
That hath eaten or drunk of the mixture,
No more than so much as a grain of wheat
And his fate shall be complete.
He will be dead in as short a while—
Less than it takes to walk a mile!

Third Rake takes and pays for the box of poison. He then goes to another house

Third Rake   I pray you sell me two large bottles of wine,
                   And an empty bottle for a need of mine.

A woman gives him three bottles. He pours poison into two of them

                   These two shall be drink for them.
                   This is mine!

Third Rake approaches the other two. Improvisation sequence in which they greet him and then stab him to death as planned

First Rake   Now let us sit and drink and make merry
                   And then we will this body bury.

They drink from the two bottles of poison and, with horrible convulsions, die

Pardoner (*preaching to the audience*)
                   O cursed sin, of all cursedness,
                   O traitors, homicides, O wickedness,
                   O gluttony, lechery and gambling.
                   Now, good men, God forgive you your trespass
                   And keep you from the sin of avarice—
                   Now ladies and gentlemen I have in my hand
                   Relics and pardons, the best in England
                   Given me straight from the Pope's throne—
                   Come forth now and kneel down,
                   And meekly receive my pardon.
                   I recommend that our host should begin
                   For he is the most enveloped in sin.
                   Come on now, you shall be first
                   To kiss the relics; unbuckle your purse.

Host   By the cross which St Helena found
                   I wish I had your coillons in my hand—
                   I would enshrine them in a hog's turd

Pardoner   I will not answer a word.

Knight   No more of this, for it is quite enough—
                   Sir Pardoner, be glad and of merry cheer,
                   And ye, Sir Host, that to me be dear.
                   I pray you, kiss the Pardoner—
                   And Pardoner, come let us laugh and play
                   And then ride forth upon our way.

They embrace and ride off

INTERLUDE

Host Now, my friends, we have travelled thus far together, through Sittingbourne and Teynham, Ospringe and Faversham, Boughton under Blee—and we are come to Harbledown where shortly we shall see the Cathedral itself wherein is the shrine of the blessed Saint Thomas. One more story shall see us there! Whose shall it be?
Various Voices The Merchant's. The Prioress's.

The Miller protests loudly

> The Reeve's.

Host   Peace! We shall never agree—
Let our audience choose and we shall see

Now in this hat shall be placed anon
The names of the other tales each one,
Now draw forth a name and we shall see
Whose tale it shall be.

The names of the tales are put in a hat and someone is asked to draw. Or some other method is devised to choose between The Nun's Priest's Tale and The Franklin's Tale. Any member of the company may relate the chosen tale

In faith it shall be the Franklin's/Nun's Priest's Tale
Now where is he, our ears to regale?

Kit
Another   *(together)*

In faith that Franklin/Priest is lost upon the way
So I'll tell you the tale he told me one day.

THE FRANKLIN'S TALE

This tale can be played like a Victorian melodrama

Narrator In Armorik, that is called Brittany,
There was a knight that loved a lady,
And many a labour he did 'ere she was won
For she was one of the fairest under the sun.
At last their minds were in accord
And she took him for her husband and her lord.
He vowed that against her will he would have no sway
And he would love and serve her night and day.

Lady Sir, since of your gentleness
You prefer me to have so free a rein,
God forbid that between us twain
Through my fault there be quarrel or strife.
Sir, I will be your humble true wife.

Wife of Bath Love is a thing as any spirit free,
Women naturally desire liberty.
And not to be constrained—as in thrall.
And so do men, if the truth I say shall!

Narrator A year or more lasted this blissful life—
But this knight, Arveragus,
Then prepared to go and dwell a year or twain
In England, that was also called Britain—
To seek glory in valiant deeds.
Now to speak of Dorigen his wife,
That loved her husband as her heart's life—
For his absence weepeth she and sighed—
She moaneth, waketh, waileth, fasteth and nearly died.
But good Arveragus in all his care,
Sent her letters of his welfare,
And that he would come quickly again—
Otherwise with sorrow she would have been slain.

Other women enter to comfort Dorigen

Now as her castle stood close by the sea
Full often on the cliffs with her friends walked she.

Dorigen (*looking out to sea*)
Alas, is there no ship of the many I see,
Which will bring home my lord?

O as I look down on those grisly black rocks,
My heart quakes—O keep my lord safe from shocks
And dangers. Would to God those black rocks
Were sunk in hell.

Woman   Come and cheer your spirits on this morn of May,
Let's dance and play in the garden all day

DANCE 3

There is a dance. Dorigen doesn't join in but stands aside. An elegant young man joins in and eventually he and Dorigen are left alone together

Young Man Madam, by God that this world made,
If I thought that it might make you glad,
I wish that on that day that your Arveragus
Went overseas that I, Aurelius,
Had gone there, never to return again.
For I see it is all in vain—
For I love you and have done so for two years,
Have mercy my sweet, I will die of my tears.

Dorigen   Is this your desire, and say ye thus—
Never before did I know this Aurelius.
By God that gave me both soul and life
I shall never be an unfaithful wife.
In word nor work, as long as I have wit,
I will be his to whom I am knit.

(Gently)

But, Aurelius, by great God above,
I would like to consent to be your love—
So, as I see you piteously complain,
On that day when with might and main
You remove all the rocks, stone by stone,
So that none is left on this shore alone—
And when you have made this coast so clean
That not one black rock is to be seen—
Then I will love you best of any man!

Aurelius   Madam, this is impossible,
Then must I die of sudden death terrible.

He strides away and then strikes a pose of despair. The women come and get Dorigen

Narrator   Arveragus, with prosperity and great honour—
As if he were of chivalry the flower,

Arveragus enters

Is comen home!
O blissful art thou now, Dorigen,
That hath thy lusty husband in thine arms!

They are totally wrapped up in each other

But two years or more lay wretched Aurelius—
Nor comfort at this time had he none,
Save from his brother, which was a scholar,
Who knew of all this woe and dolour.

Brother   It comes to my remembrance,
That while I was at Orleans in France,
Where young scholars study occult arts—
I once saw a book which imparts
The secrets of the phases of the moon.
My brother shall quickly find a cure,
For my magical illusions I am sure—
Those black rocks could disappear each one,
If we may meet some scholar of magic
My brother shall have his love.
(*He goes to Aurelius*)
Arise Aurelius, we must be gone,
To Orleans must we go anon,
And if we come there tomorrow,
You shall be released from sorrow.

They go and meet a learned-looking man

Scholar   I know the cause of your coming

They are astonished

For I know all things that have been
And are to be.
Therefore, good friends come home with me!
Let us have supper as it is best
That you amorous folk must have some rest.

They sit down and enjoy wine brought by a servant

Now, Aurelius, what will my reward be
For removing all the rocks of Brittany
And from the Gironde to the mouth of the Seine?
Less than a thousand pounds I will not entertain!

Aurelius   Fie on a thousand pound,
This wide world, which that men say is round,
I would it give if I were lord of it.
This bargain is fully driven, for we are knit,
Ye shall be paid truly by my troth.
Now look that through negligence or sloth
We tarry here no longer than tomorrow!

Scholar   Nay, I give you my word,
Upon the morrow, when that it is day,
To Brittany we shall make our way.

Narrator	This was, as my books remember, The cold, frosty season of December. The bitter frosts with the sleet and rain Brought the time of Noël again.

The Scholar sets up charts and magic circles and after much incantation and mumbo-jumbo runs to Aurelius

Thunder etc is heard

Scholar	Through my magic, for a week or two I say It seems that all the rocks have gone away!
Aurelius	What miracle is this?
Scholar	You shall live in endless bliss.
Narrator	Aurelius, who was yet in despair As to whether he would have his lady fair, Went to the church to thank the powers above And where he knew he would meet his love For since early in the day She too had gone forth there to pray.

Aurelius sets out to meet Dorigen who has been to the temple to pray. He prays too

Aurelius	I, woeful wretch, Aurelius, Thank you lord and my lady Venus That me hath holpen from my cares cold. (*He sees Dorigen*) My right lady, Whom I most dread and love as best I can— Madam, I speak it for honour of you, More than to save my heart's life true, I have done as you commanded me And if you will, you may go see— Do as you wish, have your pledge in mind, For quick or dead, right there you shall me find. It is for you to spare him who you look upon, But well I know, the rocks are gone!

He leaves. She is horrified

Narrator	He took his leave and she astonished stood— In all her face was not a drop of blood— She had never expected such a trap.
Dorigen	Alas, that ever this should hap! For wend I never by possibility, That such a freak or marvel might be— It is against the process of nature.
Narrator	And home she goeth, a sorrowful creature.

Dorigen   Alas I must choose between death or shame,
I would rather die than my body defame. (*She weeps pitifully*)

Arveragus enters and finds her

Arveragus   Why, my wife, do you weep so sore?

Dorigen   Alas, that ever I was bore—
I have promised . . . I have sworn (*She whispers urgently in his ear*) . . . I will tell you all!

Arveragus (*laughing*)
Is there ought else, Dorigen, but this?

Dorigen   Nay, nay, God help me, this it is.

Arveragus   Now, wife, let sleeping dogs lie—
Perhaps all may yet be well today.
—You must keep your promise, this I say,
For as surely as God has mercy on me,
I would rather stabbed to death be
Than have you break your word—
Truth is the highest thing that man may hold!
(*He weeps*)
But, I forbid you on pain of death
That while you have life or breath,
That to any man must you tell this misadventure,
And as best I can, I will endure.

They kiss and part

Aurelius enters and sees Dorigen walking

Aurelius   Madam, whither are you going?

Dorigen   Unto the garden, as my husband bade
There to keep the promise that to you I made,
Alas, alas.

Narrator   Aurelius was amazed at this
And in his heart had great compassion
For her and her lamentation—
And considering what was best on every side
—Whether he should with his lusts abide,
And do a deed of wretchedness
Against nobility and gentleness—
He said:

Aurelius   Madam, say to your lord Arveragus
That since I see his great nobility,
And see your great distress before me—
I would rather suffer woe
Than destroy the love which is between you two.

I release you, madam, from your bond,
Though of you I grow more fond;
I will depart—you may me dismiss—
But all wives must be careful what they promise!
Thus a squire can do a gentle deed
As well as a knight—to this take heed.

They part as she falls at his feet in thanks

Narrator   Arveragus and Dorigen his wife
In sovereign bliss now led their life—
She was to him true for evermore;
And of these two folk from me you'll hear no more!

Arveragus and Dorigen exit

Aurelius   Alas, that I promised bold
A thousand pounds of pure gold
Unto this philosopher. What shall I do?
I see that all my fortune is through.
My heritage I must sell, I fear,
And be a beggar—I cannot stay here.
But nevertheless I will assay
On fixed dates my debts to pay.
And thank him for his great courtesy—
I cannot be false, I will not lie.

He goes to his money box and takes out all he has and goes to the Scholar

Master, here is five hundred pounds,
I beg you to give me time to pay the remnant;
—I can make a vow
That I have always kept my word till now—
My debt shall be discharged, though without my shirt
I go a-begging in the dirt.

Scholar   Have I not kept my covenant with thee?

Aurelius   Yes, certainly, most well and truly.

Scholar   Have you not had your lady as thee liketh?

Aurelius   No, no—for the knight's honour me striketh—
Arveragus, of his gentleness
Would rather die in sorrow and distress
Than to see his wife to a promise be false—
And she would rather have died that day
Than be false to her husband in any way—
That made me have for her great pity,
And just as freely as he sent her to me
I freely sent her back again—
This is the sum of it, there is nor more to say.

Scholar   Dear brother
Each of you acted nobly to the other.
Thou art a squire, and he is a knight—
But God forbid, in his great might,
If a scholar cannot do as noble a deed
As either of you—now take heed.
Sir, I release thee from thy thousand pound—
And right now as if you had crept from the ground
And never before had known me—
For, sir, I will not take a penny from thee
For all my art or for my travail—
You have paid for my food and ale—
It is enough—and farewell, have good day!

Narrator   And with that he went his way.
Lordings, this question I will ask you now,
Who was the most generous—what think you—
Now tell me before we further go.
This tale's at an end—and we must know.

THE NUN'S PRIEST'S TALE

Narrator A poor widow, somewhat advanced in age
Was once dwelling in a humble cottage—
She had a farmyard enclosed all about
With stakes and a dry ditch without—
In which she had a cock named Chauntecleer:

The Cock struts in

In all the land in crowing he had no peer,
His voice was merrier than the merry organ
That plays in church.

The Cock crows loudly

His comb was redder than fine coral,
And like the battlements of a castle wall,
His bill was black, like jet it shone
Like azure were his legs and toes,
His nails whiter than lily flowers.

The Cock is vainly posing

This gentle cock had in his governance
Several hens, to do all his pleasance.

Hens cluck all round him

The one with the most beautifully coloured throat
Was called fair damsel Pertelote—

There is obvious love between them

And in those days beasts and birds could speak and sing!

Chauntecleer is on his perch with Pertelote and suddenly starts groaning

Pertelote O my heart dear,
What aileth you to groan in this manner?
You are a fine sleeper, fie for shame!

Chauntecleer Madam,
I pray you take it not agrief
By God, I dreamed I was in such mischief—
I dreamed how that I roamed up and down
Within our yard, and there I saw a hound
That tried to seize me and have me dead,
His colour was betwixt yellow and red.

> And tipped was his tail and both his ears
> With black, unlike the rest of his hairs
> His snout was small with two glowing eyes,
> For fear of his look my heart almost dies.

Pertelote   Avaunt! Fie on you faint heart!
> Now have you lost my heart and all my love,
> I cannot love a coward by my faith,
> For surely, whatever a woman saith
> We all desire brave husbands.
> How dare you say, for shame, unto your love,
> That anything might make you afeard,
> Have you no man's heart though you have a beard?
> Dreams come from over-eating or from wind—
> Now for pity sake take no notice of dreams
> But take some laxative when we fly from the beams!

Chauntecleer   Madam, I thank you for your love—
> But as for dreams read in ancient books
> How many dreams have been fulfilled—
> Nevertheless, my heart is thrilled
> When I see the beauty of thy face—
> You are so scarlet red about the eyes
> —All my dread and anxiety dies—
> For also it is certain *In principio*
> *Mulier est hominis confusio*—
> Madam, the meaning of this latin is
> "Woman is man's joy and all his bliss!"
> I am full of joy and delight!

They fly off their perch and start clucking around, pecking up grains of corn

Narrator   Now, a black-marked fox, full of sly iniquity,
> Who had lived in the wood for years three—
> Burst through the hedge and in a bed of cabbages lay
> Until the mid-morning of that day

Fox duly enters

> Women's advice is often baneful—
> It brought us first to woe,
> When Adam lost paradise we know!

Chauntecleer sees Fox and is about to run away

Fox   Gentle sir, alas where are you going?
> Are you afraid of me, your friend without knowing?
> Now certainly I would be no friend
> If I some harm or villainy intend—
> But truly, the cause of my coming
> Was only to hear how you sing—
> For truly you have a more beautiful voice

Than any angel who doth in heaven rejoice.
Both your honourable father and mother
Have been to my house—
I would love to entertain you as my brother!

And as for singing, I will say,
I never heard anyone sing the way
Your father did in the morning; his song
Was so tuneful and so strong.
He achieved this wonderful sound
By closing his eyes and standing tip-toe on the ground.
He stretched out his neck, long and small—
O please sing like that—you could do it all!

Chauntecleer experiments with these positions and suddenly Fox grabs him by the neck and runs off with him

There is a great din and Fox is chased all round the stage, and the theatre, by the rest of the cast, dogs bark, horns blow etc

Chauntecleer   Sir, if I were as you
I would say to all who pursue—
"Turn back you proud churls all
A very pestilence upon you fall!
Now I am come to this wood's side
In spite of you this cock shall here abide—
I will eat him in faith and that anon!"

Fox   In faith, it shall be done!

As he opens his mouth the cock flies out and up into a tree

Alas, Chauntecleer, alas,
I have done you great trespass,
In as much as I made you afeard,
When I took you and brought you from the yard.
But sir, I did it with no wicked intent,
Come down, and I shall tell you what I meant.

Chauntecleer   No indeed—may I be damned
Both blood and bones,
If you beguile me more than once—
No more shall you, through your flatteries
Entice me to sing and close my eyes—
For he that winketh when he should see,
In God's favour shall he never be!

Fox   No, but God give misfortune that will never cease
To those who jabber when they should hold their peace!

Fox exits

Narrator   Lo, such it is for to be reckless
And negligent, and listen to flattery—

But ye that think that this tale is a folly
About a fox and of a cock and a hen—
Taketh thou the moral, good men—
For St Paul saith, that all that is written is
For our teaching—the moral is this—
Take the fruit—but leave the chaff alone—
Now great God upon thy throne—
Make us all good men
And bring us to your bliss above, Amen.

THE MILLER'S TALE

Host	Friends, we are come to the gate of the town— Yonder stands the Cathedral, the jewel in the crown! Now before we enter I must decide Whose tale was best on our long ride.
Miller	When is my tale to be told thou scurvy knave?
Host	'Tis like to be too lewd.
Miller	Thy wit doth rave.
Moll	We cannot have Robin's tale, he hath a foul tongue.
Kit	Indeed we must, for we are young And must hear all manner of saucy tales.
Knight	We must hear his tale, or our project fails.
Miller	I will begin.
Host	No, no. To the town we must enter in. You may not tell your tale, it is too late.
Wife of Bath	Come let him tell his tale E'en here by the gate.
Pardoner	'Twill be a poor tale, I rather think He is a little the worse for drink.
Moll	I will close my ears, his brain is pickled.
Kit	Come now, we all know you like to be tickled.
Knight	Let him speak.
Miller	By God's soul, I will speak or else go my way.
Host	Tell on in the devil's name, Thou art a fool, thy wit is overcome.

One of the Women (*to the audience*)

What more can we say but that this Miller
Would not spare his words for any man
But told his tale as only a churl can—
We regret we must repeat it here.
So if your sensitivity is greater
Just leave your seat and come back later!

Host   I ask you not to put on me the blame,
                      —But then, this is really just a game.

As the Miller speaks, actors act out the story

Miller   Have you finished? Right, I shall begin.
                      Once upon a time, dwelling at Oxford
                      There was a rich churl who had guests to board.
                      And of his craft he was a carpenter.
                      With him there was dwelling a poor scholar
                      Who had studied the arts but now his fantasy
                      Was turned for to learn astrology.
                      This clerk was named pleasant Nicholas.
                      A chamber he had in that hostelry—
                      He was like a meek maiden for to see—
                      In his room lay a gay psaltery
                      On which at night he made melody.
                      And thus this clerk his time he spent
                      Depending on his friends to find the rent.

                      This carpenter had wedded new a wife
                      Whom he loved more than his life—
                      She was eighteen years of age—
                      Jealous he was, and kept her almost in a cage,
                      For she was wild and young, and he was old
                      And thought himself likely to be a cuckold.
                      Fair was this young wife, so lovely and slim,
                      Graceful and soft, elegant and trim.
                      Her eyebrows were plucked and arched high,
                      And truly she had a wanton eye!
                      She was more wonderful to see
                      Than the blossom on a sweet pear tree.

*Nicholas, who has been watching for the Carpenter to go away, creeps up
behind Alison*

Nicholas (*putting his arms around Alison and cupping her bosom*)
                      O Alison, unless of you I have my fill,
                      Sweetheart I'll die, I surely will!
                      (*Holding her hips*)
                      Darling, love me right away
                      Or I'll certainly die today.

Alison (*twisting*)
                      I will not kiss you by my fay!
                      I'll struggle 'till I get away.
                      Why, let be, let be, Nicholas
                      Or I'll yell out: Help! Alas!
                      Take away your hands, or else I'll spurn you
                      You're meddling with matters that don't concern you!

Nicholas (*smoothly*)
> Darling, have mercy on me I cry—
> Don't you long with me to lie?
> (*He tickles her neck*)
> Now come, swear on oath by St Thomas of Kent
> You will be at my commandment!

Alison gives in

Alison
> My husband is so full of jealousy
> That unless I come to you privily—
> I might as well be dead on my feet
> You really must be most discreet.

Nicholas
> Nay, thereof care thee nought,
> A clerk has used his time poorly the while,
> If he cannot a carpenter beguile!

They kiss and part. Nicholas runs to his room and strums his guitar hard

Miller
> Then it fell out that this good wife
> Went to parish church each holy day of her life
> Her forehead shone as bright as the day, as fresh as a lark.
> Now there was a young parish clark,
> And he was named Absalom.
> Curled was his hair, like gold it shone.
> A merry lad was he, or God me save.
> He knew how to let blood and clip and shave.
> In twenty ways could he trip and dance—
> On his slim legs would mince and prance—
> And sing high treble.
> On Alison he had cast his eye
> And came to her window when night was nigh.

The Carpenter and Alison are seen in bed. Absalom approaches the window

MUSIC 6

Absalom (*singing*)
> Now dear lady, if thy will it be
> I pray you now take pity on me!

Carpenter (*waking*)
> What, Alison, hearest thou not Absalom
> That chanteth under our chamber wall!

Alison   Yes, God knows I hear every bit of it.

They yawn and sleep

Miller
> From day to day this jolly Absalom
> Became in love quite woe begone—
> He worketh all the night and day
> And sent her love tokens sweet and gay.

But what availeth him in this case—
For Alison loved Nicholas.

Carpenter (*to Alison*)
My dearest, to Osney I must be gone—
I'll be back tonight—'twill not be long.

As soon as he has gone Alison signals to Nicholas who comes to her

Nicholas
Now I have devised a cunning plan
To quite deceive your foolish old man—
And if this game goes aright
You shall sleep in my arms all night!
Now I must no longer tarry
But quietly unto my chamber carry
Both meat and drink for more than a day—
And, if your husband asks for me, you must say
I must be sick.

He leaves her and takes to his bed

Alison and the Carpenter sit down together

Carpenter
I am afraid by St Thomas
That all is not well with Nicholas,
God forbid that he should die suddenly,
This world is risky certainly,
I saw a corpse being carried to church today—
Yet that man was at work only last Monday.
(*Calling the maid*)
Go up, knock at his door,
See how it is and tell me boldly.

Maid (*knocking hard*)
What! How! What do ye Master Nicholas
How may ye sleep all the day?

She looks under the door. Nicholas now sits gazing into space

Carpenter (*after looking under the door*)
This man has fallen with his astronomy
Into some fit or agony—
Get me a staff that I may underspore,
While you, my girl, heave up the door.

With a stick they heave the door off its hinges

(*Shaking Nicholas by the shoulders*)
What, Nicholas, what, look down,
Awake and think on Christ's passion.

He makes the sign of the cross and faces the corner of the house

Jesu and Saint Benedict
Bless this house every wicked wight.

Nicholas (*sighing*)
            Alas, shall all the world be lost again!

Carpenter   What? Think on God as do all men that swink.

Nicholas   Fetch me a good strong drink,
            And after will I speak privately
            Of something concerning me and thee.

The Carpenter anxiously fetches drink

            John, my host, beloved and dear,
            The end of the world is drawing near—
            Now John, I do not lie,
            I have seen in astrology
            That shall fall a rain so strong and wild,
            'Twill make Noah's flood seem mild.
            This world, in less than an hour
            Shall be drowned in this hideous shower.

Carpenter   Alas, my wife
            Shall my Alison lose her life?
            Is there no remedy for this dismay?

Nicholas   Yes, if you do just as I say!
            Go first and fetch us to this inn
            A kneading trough or tub of tin
            For each of us, but look they be large.
            So that we can use them as a barge.
            And when you have tubs for us three,
            Hang them in the roof that none may see.
            And take an axe to cut the rope
            When the rains come and away we'll float!
            Now tomorrow night we must sleep apart
            Each in our tubs, waiting for the rains to start!

Three tubs are brought and placed on a high level and fixed with rope. By candlelight Nicholas, Alison and the Carpenter creep in and each sit in a tub. They all say "hush" and the Carpenter says his prayers. The Carpenter falls asleep and Nicholas and Alison steal away to bed. There is much energetic love-making

    Absalom enters

Absalom   I have not seen John the Carpenter,
            He must be away buying timber—
            Now is the time to stay awake all night,
            And to tell Alison all I might.
            At the very least I will her kiss—
            My mouth has itched all the long day
            —I will prepare for a while and then go play!

He preens and grooms himself and take herbs to sweeten his breath.
Approaching the window, he knocks and coughs quietly

What do you honeycombe, sweet Alison—
My fair bird, sweet cinnamon.
Awake my sweetheart and speak to me
For I die of love for thee!

Alison (*coming to the window*)
Go away from my window, you fool
I love another—for you I'm cool—
Go away now, Absalom
Or I will have to throw a stone
Let me sleep!

Absalom   That ever true love was treated this way—
At least come kiss me for love of me.

Alison   Wilt thou go thy way then if you do?

Absalom   Yea, certainly, Alison, my sweetheart true.

Alison   Then make thee ready, Thou shalt kiss my cheek
I come anon—
(*To Nicholas*)
Just stay there still
And you shall laugh till you've had your fill.

Absalom (*preparing his lips*)
I am loved in all degree
For after this cometh more, you will see.

Alison (*opening the window*)
Have done, move on, speed thee fast
Our neighbours must not see this pass.

Miller   Now the night was black as coal
And at the window she put her hole

Alison sticks her bare bottom out of the window

Absalom approaches and kisses her bottom with relish, he falls back

Absalom   Fie alas, what is this
A cheek with a beard is what I kiss!

Nicholas (*laughing*)
A beard, a beard this goes well—

Absalom   I'll pay him back though I rot in hell!
(*He washes his lips, rubs them in the sand etc.*)

Miller   Softly now he crossed over the street
To the blacksmith Gervase
Who was sharpening sheers and ploughshares.

Absalom (*knocking*)
        Open up Gervase, and that anon.

Gervase   Who's that?

Absalom   'Tis I, Absalom.

Gervase   Why, Absalom why are you come so early
        Sure you've been meddling with some gay girly!

Absalom   Friend so dear
        That hot iron in the chimney there—
        Lend it to me, there is something to be done
        And I will bring it again full soon.

Gervase   Certainly were it gold
        You should have it. But what for—
        Am I to be told?

Absalom   Thereof, be as be may
        I shall tell thee well tomorrow day!
    (*He grabs it and stealthily approaches and knocks at Alison's window*)

Alison   Who is there? I warrant a thief.

Absalom   Why no, God knows my sweet leaf!
        I am thy Absalom my dearling,
        I have brought thee a golden ring.
        It is yours if you give me a kiss.

Nicholas   Now I had just got up to piss—
        I will now improve this jape,
        He shall kiss my arse 'ere he escape.
        (*He sticks his bum out of the window*)

Absalom   Speak sweet bird, I know not where thou art

Miller   At this Nicholas let forth a (*noise of a huge fart*)

Absalom sticks the hot iron on Nicholas' bum. Nicholas cries out

Nicholas   Help! Water! Help! Water!

The Carpenter wakes and pulls the rope so that his tub rocks and tips him to the floor

Carpenter   Water! Noah's flood is coming
        The flood is upon us!

Nicholas }
Alison   } (*together*) He's mad

        He's mad

Gervase   In faith be believed Noah's flood was coming!

The Carpenter goes on protesting while all laugh at him

Miller   My tale is done
               And God save all the company! (*He swoons*)

Host   Now you must assist me in this task
               Applaud as I name each tale, I ask,
               And the tale which gets the greatest applause
               Shall win for its teller bounteous stores!
               (*He names the tales in turn*)
               Friends, the ... is the winner the sooth to say
               He shall sup well this very day—
               Now come, the Tavern's doors do us invite,
               We shall have no more tales tonight.

Everyone exits except the Miller

Miller We had such sport when Master Chaucer was with us, and he wrote in his book many more of the tales we heard upon that journey! We lodged at the Inn of the Chequers of Hope—the Pardoner disgraced himself with Kit the barmaid and spent the night in a basket with Warwick the dog! But that's another story! I debated with that Pardoner the meaning of the many images in the stained glass of the Cathedral and the Knight went to inspect the town's defences! But you must read Master Chaucer's book!

The whole company enters

MUSIC 7 (reprise)

THE END

FURNITURE AND PROPERTY LIST

Only items mentioned in the text are included in this list. More (or less) properties can be used at the Director's discretion

Prologue

Signpost
Book of "The Canterbury Tales" **(Miller)**
Hobby horses **(Company)**
Baggage **(Company)**
Tankards **(Wenches)**
Benches etc
Vertical sheet
Straws **(Host)**

The Knight's Tale

Garlands
Mirror **(Arcite)**
Old clothes **(Squire)**
Money bags **(Squire, Arcite)**
Rope **(Palamon's friend)**
"Horse" **(Arcite)**
Sword **(Arcite)**
Armour, including lances **(Palamon and Arcite)**
Banners, seats **(Company)**
Gravestone

The Wife of Bath's Tale

Bed

Pardoner's Tale

Sword
Three straws
Box of poison
Three wine bottles

The Franklin's Tale

Wine
Charts, magic circles

The Miller's Tale

Guitar
Three tubs
Candles

LIGHTING PLOT

The choice of lighting is left to the individual Director

EFFECTS PLOT

Cue 1   **Knight** covers his eyes   (Page 21)
                 Wedding bells

Cue 2   **Pardoner** "... lies and dissembling!"   (Page 24)
                 Bell

Cue 3   **Scholar** runs to Aurelius   (Page 32)
                 Thunder

MADE AND PRINTED IN GREAT BRITAIN BY
LATIMER TREND & COMPANY LTD PLYMOUTH

MADE IN ENGLAND

www.ingramcontent.com/pod-product-compliance
Lightning Source LLC
Chambersburg PA
CBHW060356180626
46817CB00008B/3035